A picture of my baby goes here.

Little Simon

An imprint of Simon & Schuster Children's Publishing Division
1230 Avenue of the Americas
New York, New York 10020

Published by The Metropolitan Museum of Art and Simon & Schuster.
LITTLE SIMON is a registered trademark of Simon & Schuster, Inc., and associated
colophon is a trademark of Simon & Schuster, Inc.

Visit our Web site: www.SimonSaysKids.com

30 29 28

ISBN 978-0-684-18712-9

Produced by the Department of Special Publications, The Metropolitan Museum of Art

Printed in Italy

The drawings in this book are adapted from illustrations by Marie Madeleine Franc-Nohain
for a baby book published in Paris in 1914. The book, *Le Journal de Bébé*, is in the collections
of The Metropolitan Museum of Art.

The Elisha Whittelsey Collection, The Elisha Whittelsey Fund, 1977 1977.588.1

MMA 14-01007-8

0912 MON

MY NEW BABY AND ME

A First-Year Record Book for
Big Brothers and Sisters

by Dian G. Smith
Designed by Douglas Sardo

THE METROPOLITAN MUSEUM OF ART
LITTLE SIMON

SOME THINGS ABOUT ME

My name is _____

I am _____ years old.

The date today is _____

My birthday is _____

I am a big

☐ brother

☐ sister

These are some of the things I can do:

☐ say the alphabet

☐ ride a tricycle   ☐ ride a camel

☐ ride a bicycle

☐ bounce a ball _____ times
how many?

☐ get an allowance

☐ build a robot

☐ go down a slide

☐ do a somersault

☐ say this very long word: _____

☐ say it backward

☐ pay for something myself
I bought a _____

☐ hop on one foot _____ times
how many?

☐ rope a zebra

Here are some more things I can do:

☐ sing a song
   My favorite song is _____

_____

☐ count all the way to _____

☐ tie a knot   ☐ tie my shoelaces

☐ get dressed by myself
   My favorite outfit is _____

_____

☐ whistle   ☐ do a puzzle with_____ pieces
                                    how many?

☐ eat with a spoon and fork
   My favorite food is _____

☐ go to school   ☐ go to the movies
                         Here's a ticket stub to prove it:

☐ play a drum

☐ fly to the moon
☐ do other things, too: _____

_____

And I can draw a picture!

SOME THINGS
ABOUT MY FAMILY

This is a picture of my family.

There are _____ of us.

how many?

Our names are: _____

_____

_____

_____

_____

We live ☐ in a house   We have a ☐ dog
        ☐ in a cave   ☐ cat
        ☐ on a farm   ☐ gerbil
        ☐ on a boat   ☐ alligator
        ☐ in an apartment   ☐ fish
        ☐ in a zoo   ☐ new baby

This is a picture of Mommy just before the baby came.

Before the baby came, Mommy looked like she had swallowed
- ☐ a pillow
- ☐ a basketball
- ☐ a whale
- ☐ a million chocolate chip cookies
- ☐ _____
      something even bigger

This is where I was when my baby was born: _____

_____

This is how I was feeling then: ☐ happy
                                ☐ sad
                                ☐ excited
                                ☐ worried
                                ☐ mixed-up
                                ☐ _____
                                          something else

This is where I first saw my baby: _____

_____

My baby ☐ was
         ☐ wasn't   like what I expected.

Here's why: _____

_____

_____

My new baby is a ☐ boy ☐ girl

My baby's birthday is

My baby's name is

We picked it because _____

These are some silly names I call my baby: _____

I picked them because _____

In our family, my baby looks most like _____

Here's why: _____

_____

_____

My baby sleeps in   ☐ a cradle

☐ a tub

☐ a shoe box

☐ a bunk bed

☐ a birdcage

☐ a crib

My baby rides   ☐ in a carriage

☐ on a mule

☐ in a backpack

☐ in a helicopter

☐ in a frontpack

☐ on a bicycle

MY BABY AND ME

My baby ☐ does look like me ☐ doesn't look like me

These things are the same: _____

_____

_____

_____

These things are different: _____

_____

_____

_____

I weigh _____ pounds,
as much as a
   ☐ TV set
   ☐ toaster
   ☐ helicopter
   ☐ baby carriage
   ☐ lamb
   ☐ _____
          something else

My baby weighs _____ pounds,
as much as a
☐ rabbit
☐ feather
☐ telephone book
☐ suitcase
☐ bag of groceries
☐ _____
    something else

I am _____ inches tall,
as tall as a
☐ stove
☐ chair
☐ mouse
☐ dinosaur
☐ radiator
☐ _____
    something else

My baby is _____ inches long,
as long as
☐ a cat
☐ a baseball bat
☐ a place mat
☐ my arm
☐ my leg
☐ _____
    something else

My eyes are

_____
what color?

My nose is
- ☐ straight
- ☐ curved
- ☐ zigzagged
- ☐ big

My hair is

_____
what color?

☐ curly ☐ long
☐ straight ☐ short

This is a lock of my hair.
(Ask a grown-up to help you cut it.)

I am ticklish in the places I marked

My baby's hair is

_____
what color?

☐ curly   ☐ long
☐ straight ☐ invisible

**This is a lock
of my baby's hair.**
(Ask a grown-up to help you cut it.)

My baby's eyes are

_____
what color?

My baby's nose is
☐ straight
☐ curved
☐ drippy
☐ little

My baby is ticklish in the places I marked in red.

This is a picture of my face.

This is a picture of my baby's face.

I have _____ shoes.
how many?

My baby has _____ shoes.
how many?

I have _____ socks.
how many?

My baby has _____ socks.
how many?

I have _____ pajamas.
how many?

My baby has _____ pajamas.
how many?

I have _____ stuffed animals.
how many?

My baby has _____ stuffed animals
how many?

I have _____ books.
how many?

My baby has _____ books.
how many?

I have _____ freckles.
how many?

My baby has _____ freckles.
how many?

MANY?

I have _____ teeth.
how many?

My baby has _____ teeth.
how many?

I have _____ sisters.
how many?

My baby has _____ sisters.
how many?

I have _____ brothers.
how many?

My baby has _____ brothers.
how many?

I have _____ cousins.
how many?

My baby has _____ cousins.
how many?

I have _____ rattles.
how many?

My baby has _____ rattles.
how many?

I have _____ rattlesnakes.
how many?

My baby has _____ rattlesnakes.
how many?

This is a tracing of my hand.

☐ right
☐ left

My hand is as big as
   ☐ a jar of peanut butter
   ☐ a baseball card
   ☐ a tortoise
   ☐ a baked potato
   ☐ my baby's face
   ☐ _____
          something else

This is a tracing of my baby's hand.
(Ask a grown-up to help you trace it.)

☐ right
☐ left

My baby's hand is as big as
☐ a yo-yo
☐ a penny
☐ a hamburger
☐ a french fry
☐ my thumb
☐ _____
something else

This is a tracing of my foot.

☐ right
☐ left

My shoes are size

1	4	7	36
13	5	64	3
9	10	24	11
6	2	8	12

(circle one)

My favorite kind of shoes are

☐ sneakers _____
                what brand?
☐ sandals
☐ cowboy boots
☐ horseshoes
☐ Mary Janes
☐ _____
             something else

This is a tracing of my baby's foot.
(Ask a grown-up to help you trace it.)

☐ right
☐ left

My baby wears
- ☐ baby shoes
- ☐ booties
- ☐ penny loafers
- ☐ dollar loafers
- ☐ bare feet
- ☐ _____
  something else

My baby's foot is as long as
- ☐ a playing card
- ☐ a cracker
- ☐ a crocodile
- ☐ my foot
- ☐ my hand
- ☐ _____
  something else

Big Days
(Write in the dates.)

_____ Today my baby smiled at me.

_____ Today my baby rolled over from tummy to back.

_____ Today my baby rolled over from back to tummy.

_____ Today my baby laughed at me.

_____ Today my baby held a bottle alone.

_____ Today my baby sat up alone.

_____ Today my baby drank from a cup.

_____ Today my baby crawled backward.

_____ Today my baby crawled forward.

FIRST YEAR

_____ Today my baby's first tooth popped up.

_____ Today my baby stood up holding on

to something.

_____ Today my baby stood up alone.

_____ Today my baby walked holding on

to something.

_____ Today my baby walked holding both

of my hands.

_____ Today my baby climbed downstairs.

_____ Today my baby climbed upstairs.

_____ Today my baby walked alone.

THREE-MONTH CHECKUP

The date today is _____

My baby is 3 months old.

This is a picture of my baby.

My baby eats
- ☐ milk   ☐ bananas   ☐ cereal
- ☐ beetles   ☐ _____
                   something else

My baby takes 1 2 3 4 5 6 100 naps every day.
                        (circle one)

My baby wears 1 2 3 4 5 6 100 diapers every day.
                        (circle one)

My baby likes to watch
- ☐ Mommy and Daddy
- ☐ me sticking out my tongue
- ☐ his/her own fingers
- ☐ a mobile
- ☐ TV
- ☐ _____

something else

MAKE A MOBILE FOR BABY

Tape 2 plastic straws together in the middle to form an X. Cut out 8 shapes from brightly colored paper. Tape the shapes to threads 5 to 8 inches long, then tape the ends of the threads along the arms of the X. Ask a grown-up to hang the mobile over your baby's crib or changing table.

I can make my baby smile by _____

_____

_____

_____

_____

Three-Month Checkup

My baby likes to listen to
- ☐ records and tapes
  My baby's favorite is _____

  _____

  _____

- ☐ the vacuum cleaner
- ☐ me singing
  My baby's favorite song is _____

  _____

  _____

- ☐ the doorbell
- ☐ rattles
- ☐ _____

  something else

MAKE A RATTLE FOR BABY
Use brightly colored crayons to decorate
the back of a paper plate. Fold the plate in
half. Fill it with Cheerios. Ask a grown-up
to seal your rattle with tape.

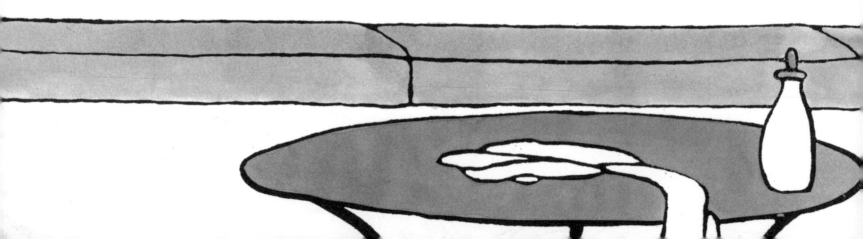

Three-Month Checkup

This is how I help the grown-ups with my baby: _____

_____

The best thing about my baby now is _____

_____

The worst thing about my baby now is _____

_____

Crying means that my baby is ☐ hungry
                                                       ☐ wet
                                                       ☐ teething
                                                       ☐ bored
                                                       ☐ tired
                                                       ☐ trying to drive me crazy

SIX-MONTH CHECKUP

The date today is _____

Today is my baby's half-birthday.

This is a picture of my baby.

My baby tries to eat ☐ food
☐ fingers
☐ keys
☐ shoes
☐ teething rings
☐ everything

I can make my baby laugh by _____

_____

These are funny faces I make sometimes.
(Draw them in.)

My baby grabs ☐ my hand
              ☐ my hair (Ouch!)
              ☐ my toys
              ☐ earrings
              ☐ plants
              ☐ everything

Six-Month Checkup

My baby hates to _____

_____

My baby likes to ☐ look in the mirror
               ☐ take a bath
               ☐ ride a motorcycle
               ☐ play games
                   My baby's favorite game is _____

_____

               ☐ watch animals
               ☐ _____
                   something else

MAKE A PUPPET FOR BABY

Find an old sock without a mate. Choose an animal you think your baby will like. Ask a grown-up to help you cut its eyes, ears, nose, and tongue out of felt. Stick your hand in the sock and glue on the pieces of felt. When the glue dries, put on a show for your baby.

Six-Month Checkup

Now I help the grown-ups with my baby by _____

_____

The best thing about my baby now is _____

_____

The worst thing about my baby now is _____

_____

When I want to get something away from my baby, I
☐ offer a toy
☐ pull hard
☐ call the police
☐ tell my parents
☐ give up
☐ _____
                                    something else

NINE-MONTH CHECKUP

The date today is _____

My baby is 9 months old.

This is a picture of my baby.

My baby likes to ☐ chew books
☐ say hi
☐ wave bye-bye
☐ fill boxes
☐ empty boxes
☐ _____
something else

My baby eats with
☐ a spoon
☐ a fork
☐ a shovel
☐ a spear
☐ chopsticks
☐ fingers

My baby eats
☐ chicken
☐ peanut butter
☐ spinach
☐ applesauce
☐ tin cans
☐ _____
              something else

This is a picture of the floor after my baby eats.
What a mess! (Draw it in.)

Nine-Month Checkup

My baby knows what I mean when I say _____

_____

When my baby says _____

    it means _____

_____

_____

What did baby say?
(Write it in.)

_____

_____

_____

_____

_____

MAKE A TAPE FOR BABY
With a grown-up's help, tape-record your baby's gurgling, cooing, crying, laughing, and talking. Add to the tape often and play it back for your baby to hear. At the beginning of each taping session, introduce yourself and your baby and record the date.

Nine-Month Checkup

I can cheer up my baby by _____

_____

My baby cries when ☐ Mommy leaves the room
                     ☐ I leave the room
                         ☐ a babysitter comes
                     ☐ I'm trying to sleep
                         ☐ it's nap time
            ☐ _____
                    something else

Now I help the grown-ups with my baby by _____

_____

The best thing about my baby now is _____

_____

The worst thing about my baby now is _____

_____

HAPPY BIRTH

Here is a picture of me and my baby
at my baby's first birthday party.

These are the people who came: _____

_____

_____

_____

_____

AY BABY!

This is what we did at the party: _____

_____

_____

This is what we ate: _____

_____

What my baby liked best was _____

_____

What I liked best was _____

_____

Here is a souvenir from the party.
(Paste it in.)

TWELVE-MONTH CHECKUP

The date today is _____

My baby is one year old.

This is a picture of my baby.

My baby walks ☐ holding my hands
☐ holding on to furniture
☐ holding a fish
☐ in a walker
☐ in a spacesuit
☐ alone

My baby can ☐ walk upstairs   ☐ crawl upstairs

My baby can ☐ walk downstairs   ☐ crawl downstairs

My baby can ☐ tie shoelaces   ☐ untie shoelaces

My baby can walk all the way from

_____

where?

to _____

where?

Twelve-Month Checkup

My baby likes to ☐ play games

        My baby's favorite game is _____

_____

☐ do mischief

        My baby's favorite mischief is _____

_____

☐ copy me   ☐ dance with me

☐ look at books

☐ pet cats

☐ _____

                   something else

MAKE A BOOK FOR BABY
Take 6 pieces of colored construction paper and fold them in half. Ask a grown-up to help you staple them together along the seam. On each page draw a picture of something your baby will recognize (a dog, a cat, a ball, or something else) or glue on pictures from a magazine. Write their names underneath if you can. Glue thin pieces of cardboard to the front and back pages for the cover. Give your book a title and read it to your baby.

Twelve-Month Checkup

Here are some of the things I've taught my baby to do: _____

_____

Now I help the grown-ups with my baby by _____

_____

The best thing about my baby now is _____

_____

The worst thing about my baby now is _____

_____

My baby can draw with ☐ crayons

    ☐ pudding   ☐ finger paint

           ☐ markers

    ☐ toothpaste   ☐ _____

                         something else

MAKE A PICTURE WITH YOUR BABY
On a day when you are drawing, give your baby a big sheet of paper and a few crayons. Babies like to copy their big brothers and sisters. If your baby doesn't understand, show baby how to hold the crayons. On the very last pages of this book you can tape in a special picture you made this year and one by your baby, too.

Next year I bet I'll learn how to

Next year I bet my baby will learn how to

- [ ] run
- [ ] kick a ball
- [ ] throw a ball
- [ ] play baseball
- [ ] skip
- [ ] throw a tantrum
- [ ] fly
- [ ] get dressed
- [ ] play checkers
- [ ] play hide-and-seek
- [ ] build a castle
- [ ] make animal sounds
- [ ] get undressed
- [ ] say my name
- [ ] drive a car
- [ ] tickle me
- [ ] say "No!"
- [ ] say "Peter Piper picked a peck of pickled peppers"
- [ ] walk forward
- [ ] make a mess
- [ ] walk backward
- [ ] run as fast as I do
- [ ] make a pile of blocks
- [ ] jump with both feet

Tape your drawing here.